What Kind of Monster?

D1487238

Mulligan was a monster.
But he didn't know what kind,
so he left the forest to find out . . .

For Ella

Copyright © 2003 by Mark Birchall.
This paperback edition first published in 2004 by Andersen Press Ltd.
The rights of Mark Birchall to be identified as the author and illustrator of this
work have been asserted by him in accordance with the Copyright, Designs and Patents Act, 1988.
First published in Great Britain in 2003 by Andersen Press Ltd., 20 Vauxhall Bridge Road,
London, SW1V 2SA. Published in Australia by Random House Australia Pty.,
20 Alfred Street, Milsons Point, Sydney, NSW 2061. All rights reserved.
Colour separated in Italy by Fotoriproduzioni Grafiche, Verona.
Printed and bound in Italy by Grafiche AZ, Verona.

10 9 8 7 6 5 4 3 2 1

British Library Cataloguing in Publication Data available.

ISBN 1 84270 318 8

This book has been printed on acid-free paper

What Kind of Monster?

Mark Birchall

Andersen Press • London

"I'm a SCARY monster," said Mulligan.
"The scariest monster ever!"
But there was nobody there,
so he went to find someone to frighten.

"GRRRAGH,
GRRRRRAGH!" he roared.

Amy wasn't a bit scared.
She gave him one of her sweets.

"Hmmm," thought Mulligan.
"If I'm not a scary monster,
I must be a MESSY monster . . .

the messiest monster ever!"

He helped Jamie mix a sticky cake . . .

Then he helped Dog dig for bones –
in FOUR different places!

And he painted some pictures
with all of his favourite colours.

But Mulligan was no messier
than anyone else,
and they got all the telling off,
which made him feel bad.

"Hmmm," he thought.
"I'm not a SCARY monster,
and I'm not such a MESSY
monster after all.
Perhaps I'm a . . .

STRONG monster . . .   But I'm not.

Or even a MAGIC monster . . .   But I'm not.

If only I was an UNDER-THE-BED
monster . . . But I'm not!

I'm not a SINGING monster,
or an ACROBAT monster . . .

. . . and I'm definitely not a
very CLEVER monster.

So what kind of monster
can I be?

I must be a BRAVE monster,
the bravest monster ever!"

So Mulligan went back
to the forest . . .

He found a deep, dark,
spooky place.
"I was right," he whispered
to himself. "I'm not even a tiny
bit frightened.
I AM a brave monster!"

Then THUD,
      THUD,
           THUD . . .

Something was coming,
something BIG!

Could it be a ghost?
A tiger?
A Tyrannosaurus REX?

Mulligan didn't feel a bit brave.
He started running, but he couldn't run
fast enough . . .

Something BIG grabbed hold of him.
It lifted him into the air.

Up,

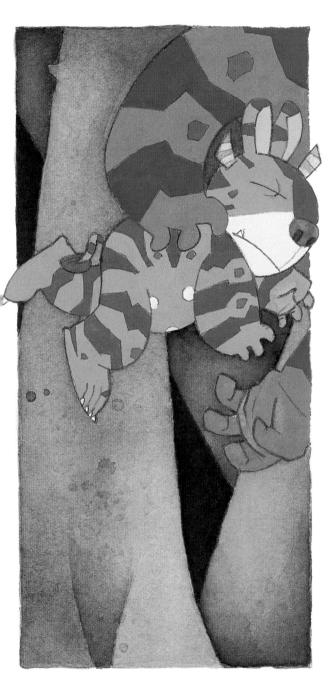

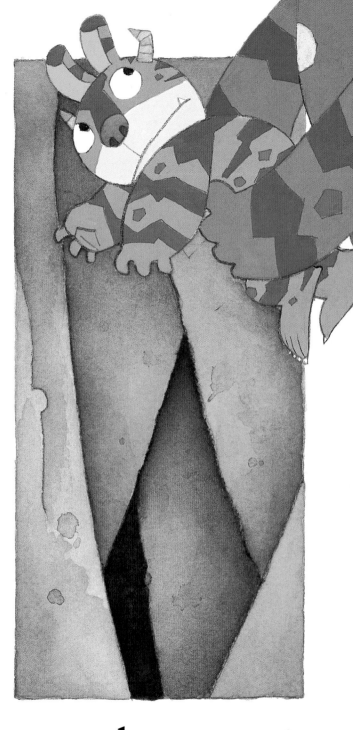

up,

up he went!
And then . . .

"Mulligan!" cried his mum. "I've looked everywhere for you. Where have you been?"

"I was trying to find out what kind of monster I am," said Mulligan sadly. "But I still don't know. I'm no kind of monster at all."

"But, Mulligan! You're my LITTLE monster," Mum told him. "My very own, NAUGHTY, LITTLE monster. The naughtiest little monster ever!"

More Andersen Press paperback picture books!

Tom's Pirate Ship
by Philippe Dupasquier

Helpful Henry
by Ruth Brown

Cat and Canary
by Michael Foreman

Tiger
by Jane Johnson

King Smelly Feet
by Hiawyn Oram and John Shelley

Millie's Big Surprise
by Gerald Rose

Super Dooper Jezebel
by Tony Ross

What Do You Remember?
by Paul Stewart and Chris Riddell

I Want To Be A Cowgirl
by Jeanne Willis and Tony Ross